Samson M. Adeyemi

-UNDISPUTED-

One man, one dream, many obstacles

Glory Awaits!

UNDISPUTED

First Published 2015 by Samson M. Adeyemi

Copyright © 2015 by Samson M. Adeyemi

Printed in the United Kingdom
ISBN: 9780992891039

Learn more information at: www.speak2samson.co.uk

TABLE OF CONTENTS

ACKNOWLEDGMENTS

I would like to thank God for the talent he has bestowed me with and all the victories he has given me in life. My gratitude goes to my late biological father- Adelabu Samuel Adeyemi, my Mum-Taiwo Adeyemi, all my sisters (Bunmi, Kemi, Bukunmi & Deborah) and my brother, Timothy.

I also want to thank my Pastor Chris Oyakhilome, Pastors Chuka and Val Ibeachum for bringing me up in the way of the Lord. Huge thanks to all my friends who have supported me and have been there for me during challenging times. This book is for you. I love and appreciate you so much.

Foreword

By the Editor - Nicola Blake

I was extremely surprised and honored when asked to write the Foreword for this book.**Undisputed**... One man, one dream, many obstacles, Glory Awaits!

This book is one of strength, courage, vision and obtaining goals. Everyone goes through challenges in life, some more than others, but it is what one chooses to do when faced with those challenges that matters. The main character of this book depicts a young man of immeasurable strength; the challenges he faced in his early years would have brought most men to a standstill, however he fought, he pushed and he persevered. The author, Samson M. Adeyemi, has allowed us to take a journey with 'Duro' through the joy of love, the pain of lost, and the disappointment of putting your trust in men. But we have also journeyed with him through the joy of God, the comfort of God and the victory in putting your trust in God.

This book lets you know that when you set your eyes on the prize, no matter what obstacles may come in your way, do not lose sight of that goal, stay focused, and push through. It lets you know that all things are possible...

Samson Adeyemi...Speaker, Advocate for young people, Visionary, Author! Has achieved so much at the tender age of 24. He has overcome many obstacles and challenges in his own life and he has used the gift that God has given him to be the voice of encouragement to others. He is a young man that gives hope to not only young people, but to people of all ages. Samson has used what he has learned so far in life to motivate him to put pen to paper which has produced an inspirational piece of work. His Faith, his strength and his love for God has always brought him to victory and the birth of 'Undisputed'...the story of 'Duro' is one that proves that. This book is a must read!

I am honored to be a part of this project, but I am even more blessed to know Samson Adeyemi personally.

Nicola Blake
Editor

Chapter 1

'Boss' the famous street dog roamed around the stinky clogged up gutters of Ejigbo Lagos, Nigeria. Everyone knew Boss; he was like the local celebrity. Both children and adults loved to play with him and were enamored by this dog who seemed to be of the human race. Boss was very fond of his best friend and owner Duro. There was a certain level of respect and love between them that most could not understand, and because of that understanding, Boss knew that Duro often struggled to look after him properly; and he also knew that even though it was an issue for Duro to look after him, Duro did not want to let him go. They had come too far and parting was not an option. So to take some of the pressure off Duro, Boss knew to look around for his own daily necessities. Duro had always lived in Ejigbo. He grew up with his grandmother, Mama Ajibade. The history of his parents were never really told to him and when little was said-, it was never straight forward and because of that, his interest in wanting to know what happened to his parents eventually waned. After all, his grandma had done a great job looking after him over the years; she really had done the best she could.

As they say "beauty is in the eyes of the beholder"; and to the residents of Ejigbo, it was beautiful, it was their territory, their domain and no one could take that from them.
Duro attended Ejigbo Model College, a state school (nothing compared to the westernized state school standard). Although he lived in the same local government, he had nothing less than fifty minutes of walking to and from school. It was not too much to ask of a 15 year old who was getting ready to sit for his final exams. Carrying your own chair to school was also the norm as no student was willing to risk the theft of their chair or sit on window frames to take dictations from teachers who were not very happy. Desks were a luxury;

and that was one luxury that they thought the students could do without. Getting through school lessons were almost a mission. It was almost a miracle to hold at least two successful lessons without student disruptions, teachers' absence, or any other inconsequential reasons that would develop and was unexpected from a school of such standard. Students seemed to be more learned in rumour and local gossip than they were of anything relating to their subjects. Mr. Okon, the school principal was almost worshiped by parents as they saw him as the one who helped shape the lives of their children. Little did they know that he had no interest in their children's development, whether academically or otherwise. Mr. Okon had control over school funds which somehow seemed to be invisible to the school Finance department itself. It was believed that his five-storey house in Umahia, Abia State (in the Eastern part of Nigeria) seemed to take shape while the school he headed lost its shape. When questioned, he would blame the Accounts Department for mismanagement of

9

funds, fire everyone in the department and employ a whole new staff who dared not question him. He was subject to no law, He was the law.

Mr. Okon's terrible management of school funds led to poor educational standards for the students and even the best students never achieved beyond a grade C in major subjects. They longed for a saviour, someone who would put them first, someone who would care enough to make sure that they received the education that they deserved, but none came, and it seemed pointless to continue to hope. Duro's West African Exams drew close and the nerves began to kick in. He didn't know what to expect, especially since they hadn't even covered half of the curriculum. Other students in private schools were already working with past exam papers individually. The only ones he had seen was the ones in the teacher's staff room which students were warned not to touch. Exams were barely two months away and failure seemed to be knocking on Duro's door.

For those students in senior secondary school three (SSS3 as it is called), days leading to the first set of exams are often very sacred. There was no time to joke now. They studied harder, prayed harder and the local libraries were often packed out with students doing last minute revision. The West Africa Senior School Certificate Exams (WASSCE) were just around the corner and for the first time, Duro was starting to feel very confident. He had made it his mission to get his hands on as much past exam papers as he possibly could, which he borrowed from friends and neighbours who went to private schools and needless to say, he revised every chance he got. . The first exam this year was Mathematics, a general paper which was compulsory for all candidates.

The first day of exams finally came and Duro had mixed feelings of both excitement and nervousness; on one hand he felt ready for his exam, but he was also worried that he would not remember all he had revised.

The day was finally here. Duro, left his house a little later than usual that morning and because of that he had to walk at a faster pace. After walking for a few minutes, he felt as if he was being followed and looking behind him, he realised that Boss, his dog was indeed the one following him. He stopped and Boss also stopped; he told Boss to go back home but Boss had his own agenda. He waited for Duro to take a few steps and he also

took a few steps; they played the stop and go game for a while. Realising that he was not going to win at this game, Duro continued hurrying to school afraid of being late. Confident that Boss would not come through the school gates and that he knew his way back home, Duro decided that it was fine that he followed and kind of welcomed the company. Reaching the school gates, Duro ran ahead. He did not want to arrive late for his exam nor did he want to miss Mr Okon's exam pep talk. Students who missed the talk the year before got into big trouble.

As Duro crossed the road leading to his school gate, he heard a screeching sound behind him from a vehicle that suddenly came to a halt. He didn't think much of it until he heard shouts and screaming from passers-by. He stopped and looked behind him and saw something moving and struggling helplessly in the middle of the road. He looked a bit closer and what he saw made him freeze in his tracks; he saw from afar that Boss had been hit by a hit and run driver and it looked as if it was Suraju's transport bus that had hit him. Suraju was a well-known reckless Danfo driver who drove one of the famous yellow and black striped Lagos buses. His bus was a rickety patched up vehicle whose brakes hardly worked and it was his only means of survival. Suraju didn't bother stopping to see what had happened to Boss he drove off as quickly as he stopped He didn't seem moved by what had happened at all and it was a certainty that he had probably hit a few dogs in his time.

As Duro stood and summarised all that had happened, he was torn between making a decision. His exam was in a few minutes and Boss needed him at this crucial time. Go back to check on Boss or go for his maths exam...? He saw Mr Okon in the distance, walking towards the exam hall. As Duro looked back and forth, warm tears freely flowed from his eyes. He thought within himself, "this exam marks the beginning of a new phase in my life"; his future depended on it. He made the toughest decision of his life at that time. He headed for the school gates and ran as fast as he could into the exam hall. He made it in just before Mr Okon arrived. Mr Okon walked in in his famous white short sleeved shirt tucked into brown chino trousers held unto his shoulders by colour coordinated brown braces. To go with his outfit was his shoes for special occasions; the pointy leopard skin ones with metal soles. He claimed the Lagos State Governor gave him those shoes as a gift for his excellent work in the school and he only wore them on special days of which the start of the final year exams seemed to be a special occasion for him.

He started his pep talk in the usual manner, by saying the same things he said every year. He then ended his talk with the only positive statement he has ever probably said to the students in the history of running the school... "and may God crown all your efforts with success". After which all the students were compelled to say "Amen, thank you Mr Okon".
He walked away making noise with his metallic shoe soles as they hit the dusty concrete floor.

Exam had begun!
The supervising teachers gave out the answer booklet whilst the exam board invigilators handed out the exam paper. It was announced that the students had an hour and forty five minutes to complete the exam and they could turn the exam paper over and start the exam.

Throughout the first 30 minutes of the exam, Duro struggled to concentrate. The thought of what had just happened to Boss disturbed him terribly. After some time, he settled down and concentrated on the questions in front of him. He seemed to be speeding through the questions. He surprisingly found most of them easier than he expected. However there were the odd questions which posed a challenge for him; he attempted them anyway and gave it his best shot. To his surprise he finished all the questions with ten minutes to spare and did not realise this until the invigilator announced "ten minutes to go". He looked through his work one more time, stood up and walked forward to hand in his answer booklet. He was asked if he had definitely finished and he answered "yes sir". As he walked out the door, he could hardly keep himself from running all the way to the school gates; as he approached the gates to the school, he no longer thought of the trouble he might get into for running on school grounds, he took off running with only one thing on his mind. He ran out of the gates heading straight to the spot where Boss' tragedy happened earlier that morning. He hoped that someone had been kind enough to help Boss. He had a tiny bit of hope that Boss might still be alive.

As he approached the scene, Duro didn't care about the approaching vehicles making sounds with their car horns. He was welcomed by the stinking, horrific sight of Boss mashed up unto the muddy road surface. No one had helped him and it seemed as if even more vehicles had driven over him and flattened his body unto the pavement even more. Duro felt so hurt. It was as though a dagger had been pierced through his chest. He knelt there for a few minutes with tears streaming down his face as vehicles drove past him pressing their horns for him to get out of the road. After a while, he got up and stood staring down at Boss with his school shirt drenched in tears and his hands wet from drying his eyes unsure of what to do next. He was eventually pulled aside by an elderly lady, a friend of his grandma who walked him home.

Chapter 2

On getting home, his Grandma, Mama as she was so fondly called, could not believe the state that he was in. She had never seen him like that. She initially thought that the exam had gone terribly wrong, but after she sat him down and dried his eyes, he explained to her what had happened. When Mama didn't see Boss that morning she assumed that he had wondered away for a bit as he often did. After listening to Duro, Mama was saddened and she knew it would take a while for Duro's heart to heal. The neighbourhood would miss Boss. Duro had lost his best friend. She encouraged him not to let what had happened affect his preparation for the rest of his exams. She even advised him to focus and do well in his exams in honour of his friend, Boss.

A few hours later, Mama offered him his favourite dish 'Amala and efo riro' but Duro had no appetite. Nothing was good enough to cheer him up. He sat on the floor in his room until he eventually dozed off. He allowed himself the escape of sleep in hopes that all he had experienced earlier in the day would all be a big dream when he woke up.

Later that evening, Mama woke him up so he could get some studying done, as she knew he had another exam the next day. Prior to his studying, she made sure he had something to eat. As he sat eating, she kept looking at him and contemplating whether to disturb him knowing how important it was that he was finally having something to eat; making a decision, Mama pulled one of the brown wooden chairs in the living room closer to Duro's chair. Duro looked up at her expectantly. He knew that whenever she makes those kind of chair pulling moves, she was about to say something really important. The last time that chair was pulled like that, it was when she told him his grandpa, Papa as he was fondly called, had died whilst he was in a coma. Now Duro was worried about what he would be told this time. Whatever it was, he was not ready for it.

Mama stared into his eyes with her hands on his shoulders. He held the mould of 'amala' as he waited for the first words to come out of her mouth. If there was some suspense soundtrack playing in the background, it would be a scene in a typical Nigerian home video. She began her talk with her usual start up lines "my son, I have something important to tell you..."

Duro's heart raced even faster now. He wasn't ready for any more bad news. He had already had a very rough day. She pulled the chair even closer now. "Do you remember what today is?" she asked, Duro looked away from Mama's eyes towards the ground. He thought for a couple of seconds and responded "Errm no I don't Mama".

"Okay no problem" Mama responded. She then continued. "You know, before your granddad died we agreed not to tell you this until you got to a particular age. I know your day has been a very tough one, but I just feel that I should let you know this information now." Duro stopped eating at this point and paid full attention to what Mama had to say. This was all very difficult for Mama, but she knew she had to tell him. She couldn't turn back now, so she proceeded; "we really never got to tell you the full story about your parent's death. All you know till now is that they passed away when you were a child. How that happened, we never told you." Duro sighed as he knew this was only going to get worse. He then interrupted her "Mama, I don't think I'm ready for this right now. I have an exam tomorrow. I don't think I can handle this right now." She put her hand on his shoulder to stop him. She then continued "Listen my son, it's too heavy a burden carrying it in my heart all this time and not telling you. The earlier I get it out of me, the better. I'm getting older and weaker by the day and who knows, I may not be around for much longer. So please hear me out." Duro with his head in his hands answered "Alright Mama". She carried on "It was a Friday night, a few weeks after you were born, your father had just arrived home from a business trip and he was well known in the area as a successful business man. He tried to keep his work a secret but his success was noticed by all. As you know, in this area of the world where we live not everyone is in support of one's success. In fact most people often look for how to bring those who are successful down to their level. My son, it was a set up by one of your father's business competitors. Your Dad was awarded several contracts which this man wanted so badly. On many occasions, he had even challenged your dad physically. But this time, he decided to take matters into his own hands. He knew your Dad was in the area, so he sent hired assassins. The plan was to threaten your Dad but your Dad wasn't a softy either, he got into a physical struggle with them when they broke into the house and they shot him in the head. He died on the spot, didn't make it to the hospital. As Duro listened, his eyes reddened, he shivered as he felt distress and anger at the same time. It was as though he was listening to the narration from a horror movie. Mama could see he was getting tense as he ground his teeth while he listened. But she had to go on...She had to continue "Your Mum was home at the time and was a witness to what happened; she screamed so loud when she saw what was happening. Those non entities knew that her shouting would draw unwanted attention, so again they pulled the trigger. She was badly injured. After the hooligans escaped, the police were called in but they had stupid excuses as to why they could not come on time. All that time, you were in your parent's room sleeping." Duro's hands trembled uncontrollably. Tears were beginning to whelm up now. He felt very troubled. Mama adds "I know how you feel but I just have to finish. The neighbours who heard the gun shot and heard the screeching wheels from the escape vehicle, went to your house. Your Mum was struggling in the pool of blood from her and your Dad. They tried taking her to the hospital but she did not make it. She took her last breath at the very entrance of the hospital. The neighbours who knew me sent someone to this house to inform Papa and I of such tragedy. It was a shock to us. We hurried there immediately. I never thought for one second that I would have had to bury my own daughter. It was a very difficult time for me. It's still very hard to deal with." In a shaky voice with saliva dribbling from his mouth from crying uncontrollably, Duro asked "So what happened to those guys and to the man who sent them?" Mama replied "Only God knows my son, the justice system of this country as at then was twisted, when it got to court, he somehow was able to lie and bribe his way out of the situation." Everyone knew it was him. Maybe he didn't mean to kill anyone, but why did he send men with guns if that was not his intention? Those he spoke to in confidence about his intentions later leaked his secrets after they fell out with him. Anyway, it was thrown out of court as a common robbery incident that got out of hand. The hooligans he sent were never found not to mention them being tried."

"But Mama why is life so unfair?" he asked. "My son, I wish I had an answer." She replied then carried on. "So your Grandpa and I had to come and pick you up. We got people to clean up the house. After which your Dad's family began their own war on who will inherit what from what your Dad had left behind. They left you with absolutely nothing." Duro at this point had no words, words failed him. His head was down now. His head and hands drenched in sweat. He somehow found strength to get up and stormed to the room that he shared with Mama. He covered himself under the bed sheet and sobbed for an unmentionable amount of time. Mama left him alone for a while but she felt relieved that she had finally told him. She felt drained but this was a burden that she carried around with her for such a long time; a sorrow that she has had to deal with over the years. But it was fresh information for Duro, and she knew it would take him some time to heal.

Around 8.30pm that evening there was a knock on the door. Mama answered the knock and it was Oluchi at the door. Oluchi was Duro's neighbour. Oluchi went to a private school and she often came to see Duro and to give him some past exam papers. Her parents could afford to pay for her to attend a private school; Sometimes she and Duro would revise together at her house as they had a power generator for electricity whenever there was power failure in the area. Consistent electricity supply was a luxury for a lot of people in Ejigbo. Oluchi's Dad was not very fond of Duro coming around. He didn't want his daughter to have anything to do with a pauper as it were. His wife however seemed to be a bit more understanding. She simply saw two good friends helping each other out. When Oluchi came to knock on Duro's door, she knelt down to greet Mama as she always did. Mama tapped her on her shoulder and warmly welcomed her in.

Oluchi asked Mama for Duro's whereabouts and Mama told her that he was in the room taking a nap. She sat down as she waited for Mama to go into the room to wake him up. Duro woke up very grumpy and in no mood whatsoever to do any kind of revision. But he had an exam the next day and if he wanted to do well as he planned, he would need to do a couple more hours of revising to help brush up on certain areas. After saying hello to Oluchi, he went back to the room to get his study materials. There was a loud banging noise on the front door. Mama was startled and reluctantly opened the door. A man barged in shouting "where's my daughter?" Oluchi recognised her father's voice straight away and made her way to the door. "Dad I only came to revise, Mum allowed me to come". "Will you keep quiet; I don't want any child of mine associating with mere commoners like these ones" he shouted. Mama looked at this man in disbelief. She could not believe what she was hearing. She felt herself getting upset at this point but she kept her calm. Oluchi's Dad grabbed his daughter's arm and stormed out. As Duro gathered his things, he heard shouting from the other room and came out. He noticed that Oluchi was gone and asked Mama what happened? She explained to him that Oluchi's father had come for her. Looking at Mama, Duro suspected that there was more to the story than what was being said. Well, Mama held the belief that Oluchi's dad knew Duro's Dad when he was alive and they were not friends as such-They were more like business competitors. Rumour has it that he may have had some hand in the assassination of Duro's Dad. Who knows, maybe guilt or just shear hatred was what he still had for Duro's Dad which probably led to him not wanting his kids to have anything to do with Duro-an offspring of his supposed 'enemy'.

Just when Duro thought he was starting to deal with the tragic story of his parent's death, Oluchi's Dad's action didn't seem to help matters at all. Nonetheless, he had an exam the next morning; he got on with his revision.

After a couple of weeks of late night revising, staying late at the local library, forgetting to eat sometimes, running around to borrow past exam papers and countless times dozing off whilst revising textbooks with the kerosene-lit lantern burning, the exam season started to draw gradually to a close.

Duro dreaded what was believed to be the Godfather of science in his school, Physics. This happened to be the last exam. He was going to put his heart and soul into this. Mama didn't trouble him much. She just left him to carry on with his studies. She didn't need to remind him to study any longer. This boy was hungry for success. They hardly had much time to talk aside from the hellos and goodbyes they exchanged when he popped out and back into the house.

The day for the highly anticipated 'almighty Physics' exam finally came. Duro was running late that morning. However, he didn't panic. He felt ready for this exam. He had done every past exam paper he could lay his hands on. He had memorised all the formulas he needed. He had prayed. He was super ready. As he left for his exam, he shouted 'Mama I'm leaving, bye'. She did not reply. She probably was still asleep. He walked at the fastest pace possible to school. He was not going to be late for this one. He needed to make use of the minutes allocated for the exam. Aside from a few questions that might pose to be a challenge, he felt he was more than ready. As this was the last exam for the students. Mr Okon was back again for his end of exam speech. He came in just five minutes to the end of the exam. He paced around the exam hall with his famous shoes. As his footsteps drew closer to certain students, their sweat glands went into overdrive, they started to sweat profusely. Mr Okon knew a lot about Physics although he never actually taught a class. As he got closer to the students, he would look at their answer booklet. For some, he would shake his head and kiss his teeth, for others, he would give them a pat on the back. No one knew which of these gestures they would receive, so a wave of panic spread through the room. Before he could go round each student, the time was up and he gave his concluding speech to the extremely nervous students who hoped he would not expose any possible error they may have made in the exam. After his speech, the students left the hall. Some went straight to the local restaurant, some to the drinks joint, some others just gathered in groups on the school field signing their school uniforms and writing good bye messages. They would not see each other for a long while.

Duro couldn't wait to catch up with Mama and tell her how his exam went and probably start eating properly again and maybe start to get some sleep. He had some time on his hands now. He could help Mama sell at the weekend open market and bring in more income.

After saying his farewell to his friends he started to make his way home. As he got closer to his house, some of his neighbours were staring at him in the most unusual manner. Others just shook their head at him as if they were pitying him. It was very strange. It felt weird. On reaching the front of his house, he noticed an unusual crowd gathered and people coming in and out of his house. He knew something was wrong. But there were no fire, no flooding, and no police around, so it couldn't have been robbers either. What on earth could have happened? He pushed through the crowd and noticed people crying and shouting. He finally got through his door. Mama laid on the bed looking lifeless. He approached the bed, with his heart racing, and his feet trembling, looking at Mama on the bed he reached out and lifted her hand, as he let go of it, it dropped back to the bed. Her face was cold. She must have been gone a long while. If Duro's world was not already crumbled, now it definitely was. No one to turn to! Thank God his exams were over. If not, there was no way he would have been able to cope with any upcoming exam. The neighbours around him tried to comfort him at the time. But no amount of comfort or words of condolences would help at that time. It was one of those times where he literally wished it was all some bad dream. How could he carry on? Just when he thought he had some time on his hands now to finally help and support Mama, she was gone!

Never to be seen again. House rent to pay, how will he feed himself? Who can he turn to? Could there be any more hope? These were some of the many questions he pondered upon as he rolled and cried on the floor in his sweat-covered shirt.

Chapter 3

Extended family members soon started to arrive and they moved Mama's body to the nearby mortuary. Mama had literally no valuable possession that the family members could fight over. Duro's Mum was Mama's only child, so there was no maternal uncle or aunty to look after Duro. After spending nights at various family members' homes, they finally decided to have a meeting to discuss the next move for him and what would happen with him. No one was ready to take full responsibility of a teenage boy. Everyone felt that they already had enough on their plates to deal with.

It was a very wet Saturday morning. The night before, Duro forced himself to sleep despite staying hungry for the whole day. The last thing he wanted was to be woken up by a loud bang on his front door. He jumped out of bed to find out who it was. It was the landlord- 'Baba Landlord' as he was famously called in the area. He came to harass Duro for the rent. If you knew this guy, you knew that he did not joke with his money. It was just two months after Mama's death and Baba landlord had made it a compulsory duty to come every week asking for his rent to be paid, or else he will be thrown out. Fair enough, it was his property but all that threat was too much for a 15 year old to handle. After several shouts and threats, he tried to show Duro who was boss. He barged into the room to look for any valuable item but there was nothing much left. Whilst he looked through things, some of the neighbours overheard what was happening and eventually came to Duro's rescue. They pleaded on his behalf and Baba landlord calmed down a bit. He gave Duro a final warning to make sure he paid up in seven days or else the streets would be his new home. Duro had had enough. He could not ask more of his already helpful neighbours whom themselves were struggling to make ends meet. Oluchi was not allowed to see him; he knew that she would have been of some help to him. He had sold most of the valuable things in the house to feed himself. Nothing much left to do.

He decided to speed up this family meeting which was meant to hold a long while back. He embarked on a long walk to one of his elderly very distant 'uncles' - Elder Olu. He wasn't really an uncle, but one of those elderly men in the family whom you are not really sure how you are related but you know you are related somehow. Elder Olu watched as Duro approached soaked through from the rain fall and trying to clean his mud covered rubber sandals as he bowed to greet him, then he dropped to the ground. The next few minutes was filled with uncertainty and total chaos. Elder Olu called for help, blew some air over him using his newspaper, turned Duro around and tried to help him open his eyes.

People came running at the cry for help and seeing Duro in that state, begun to hurry to get some water poured on him. Duro eventually opened his eyes a couple of seconds later. He was led to a chair and offered something to eat. You could see hunger in Duro's eyes. He had gone without food for a long while and even clean water was gradually becoming a luxury for him.

Elder Olu saw that help needed to come sooner than he planned. So an emergency family meeting was called to discuss the way forward for this young man. Some hours later, family members began to arrive one after another, soon enough everyone was present and the meeting commenced. It was a meeting Duro dreaded. Decisions made at this time would affect his present and future a great deal. Would things turn out for good? These were some of his many thoughts as he turned his neck, left, and right, to the corner...just to make sure he didn't miss any point, opinions and concerns raised. It was a very long four hour meeting with plenty clashes of opinions. As per tradition, Duro was not allowed to utter a word whilst the elders spoke. He could only speak when they had finished talking, and that was if they wanted to hear him speak at all. Elder Olu drew the meeting to a close and as the eldest in the family, he picked different points from what they had all said and helped to decide what he felt was best for Duro. The meeting ended, a decision was made for him but they could tell that it just didn't sit well with him. He was itching to speak. He raised his hand several times. He almost broke protocol by wanting to interrupt a few times. He was ignored; after-all, he was only a child, and what does he know? They thought. Despite the tradition, Elder Olu could see Duro's eagerness to speak. He then said "Duro, would you like to say anything?"

Duro went on his knees as a sign of respect whilst talking to the elders. "Please please please,

I don't want to live with Aunty Funke." They were all startled as to why he would say that. She lived in London after-all, what better life could he want? Any one of them would happily send their child to live with her they thought. On the outside, it all seemed like a perfect plan. But no one knew Aunty Funke better than Duro's late grandma. She knew the dirty secrets no matter how much Aunty Funke tried to cover it sometimes, Mama was her confidant. Duro overheard their conversations during the time Aunty Funke came to visit Mama whenever she was around in Nigeria. She and Mama fell out after Mama warned her sternly that if she did not withdraw from her dodgy dealings, she did not want to have anything to do with her. She loved Mama but since she was not ready to give up the dodgy dealings, she never visited again and lost communication with Mama and Duro; he hadn't seen Aunty Funke in a very long time. To the rest of the family Aunty Funke was a very successful London based business woman. To

Duro, she was a London based dodgy lady. But he couldn't tell them that. If they found out and he eventually goes to her, misery would be nothing compared to the kind of life he would live. When they asked him why, he answered "I just don't please. Anywhere else will do". People shook their head in pity thinking he was some ungrateful orphan. Elder Olu then said "listen my son, as they say, a beggar has no choice. So, you will live with Aunty Funke because we say so. She will be in Nigeria next month. Before then, we will speak with her to sort out all you need to stay with her. She is your only hope and that's final". As the meeting ended and everyone left, the words of elder Olu resounded in his mind "a beggar has no choice..." To think that he was now being compared to a beggar made his heart sink even deeper. "Could it get any worse than this?" he asked.

Later that evening, he was instructed to go back home, put all his belongings together and move to

Elder Olu's house pending the time Aunty Funke would visit Nigeria. Elder Olu's house wasn't particularly a palace; his living condition was questionable-he had 12 children of his own and three wives who all lived in his 2 bedroom apartment...squashed in like sardines. At night, the sitting room was converted to a bedroom. They barely survived from day to day; however someone had to take care of Duro temporarily and as the oldest of the remaining of Duro's extended family; he had to take on that responsibility.

Chapter 4

Aunty Funke's visit to Nigeria was highly anticipated by most of the family members. They knew she often brought gifts and money as a result of her supposed 'many businesses' which she had established in London. Duro was not looking forward to this visit at all; he hoped it would never happen. Soon weeks turned into days and days into hours and she finally arrived. She arrived in a prestigious high class car with tinted windows. She often hired different luxury cars whenever she visited. She always wanted to make an impression. Her arrival was heralded from her very entrance into the street. She even hired private security that formed an entourage as she drove into the street. This was a rare sight in that area where bicycles and maybe a few rickety cars were the norm of the day. The children playing outside chased after this vehicle, singing and clapping to welcome whoever was in the vehicle driving into their street. Hopefully something good would come out of their cheers and welcome. People looked through their windows to see who this supposed 'celebrity' was. Grown men and women ran out of their homes to follow this vehicle and see where it would eventually stop. After a couple of minutes' driving into the street, the cars eventually stopped in front of Elder Olu's compound. The following crowd stopped too and watched to see this dignitary. Elder Olu, his wives and children came out as Aunty Funke came out of her chauffeur-driven car. Even her door was opened for her. The only thing missing in this whole set up was a red carpet. It may as well have been the arrival of a celebrity to a movie premiere. The crowd of cheering children who had followed the car hoped that it was their lucky day. Aunty Funke looked at the children, and gave the eldest ones amongst them some cash to buy biscuits and sweets for everyone to share. The kids shouted in excitement and thanked her numerous times as they headed for the shops. She was welcomed into the house whilst her entourage waited outside.

She was offered all kinds of dishes even those which they would only normally eat during Christmas time or a major celebration. Duro sat there in the corner of the room knowing that Elder Olu had borrowed money to make sure that they were able to provide all these things. Even the house had a new carpet. All of these were in the hope that through their hospitality they would be rewarded with some money in return. There wasn't enough food for everyone to join in the eating. Only Aunty Funke and Elder Olu ate whilst others excused them. When they had finished, some of the children came to clear the plates giving them a chance to battle for the remnants on the plates. Duro was later called into the room to be a part of the conversation with Aunty Funke.

In all honesty, he felt it was not really a conversation as he barely had the chance to speak. It was more of instructions, decisions being made for him and just for him to say yes Ma and yes Sir to all those instructions. I mean, what does a 15 year old know? They thought again. Aunty Funke was right there this time, so Duro didn't want to say he did not want to go with her. She actually was extra nice on this day. She gave Duro some money which Elder Olu offered to 'keep safe' for him. She promised Duro that she would take very good care of him and he could even make some money by working in one of her companies. He would study in any school of his choice, he will have his own room, have a private tutor, eventually go to university and live a sweet life with her in the UK. Elder Olu's eyes lit up as she made these offers. He wished that it was one of his kids who had this opportunity of a lifetime. Duro looked very skeptical about this whole thing; it was so hard for him to trust her. His gut instinct was not to believe a thing she said. Elder Olu danced round the room like a little child and thanked Aunty Funke for having a heart of gold. Duro didn't want to look ungrateful, so he joined in too and thanked her for such generosity. However, even though he wanted to turn down the offer, but he didn't. He was mindful of his manners and finally spoke up. He stated that his results day was in the coming weeks, but Aunty Funke was leaving in two days' time. He would miss his results day, and he asked if they could travel after he received his results. Elder Olu assured him that he would pick his results up for him and post it to him in the UK. He even brought up the fact that he wanted to attend Mama's burial and be part of the planning. But still, that was not enough to convince them. He was reminded that Mama was dead and that he must move on with his own life and focus on his future and that he shouldn't worry, the rest of the family will take care of Mama's funeral. The conversation ended with Duro being told not to bother packing up anything as she will buy him new things when they arrive in the UK. She gave Elder Olu some money and some gift items for his wives and children. As she left, everyone waved to her whilst she drove to her hotel where she spent the next few days before her return to the UK.

For the next couple of days, Duro had mixed feelings. He remembered Aunty Funke's dodgy dealings. But she sounded very different in person. Is she a changed person now? Trust her this time or to remain cautious? The UK is a place where he would know no one else besides her. He had to prepare his mind for this new chapter in his life ...whatever it may be. Despite the doubts, he was ready to take this risk.

Duro's flight had to be delayed by five more days after Aunty Funke's departure. After a long six hour flight, he finally arrived at Heathrow Airport, London. Duro was awake every second of the flight. As this was his first time on a plane, he was not going to miss a thing. On his arrival, he expected to be met by Aunty Funke at the arrivals reception area. However, she wasn't there. Duro started to panic. He was in a strange new country all by himself with no phone number to contact anyone; he did not even have an address on him even if he were to make his own way. After several hours of Duro waiting, a taxi arrived and the driver walked through holding Duro's name on a card. By this time, he was cold and hungry. Now, the doubts began to run through his mind. He was there now. No turning back. Was this the worst decision he had made to date? Are things about to get worse? He walked towards the taxi driver and introduced himself. The taxi driver asked if he had been waiting for long. Duro explained how he had been waiting since the early hours of the morning. The taxi driver felt sorry for him but he explained that he came just as he got a call from Duro's aunty. He still had his doubts but he thought maybe his aunt was busy with her many business dealings. But could she be that busy to forget that he was arriving. I mean, she booked the flight and all, how could she forget? He thought to himself.

Chapter 5

On arrival to Aunty Funke's house, his eyes moved around like some rotating security CCTV camera looking at everything in sight. He noticed a young lady sitting by the computer in the sitting room. Aunty Funke introduced him to her daughter, Maria who was about 2 years younger than Duro. Duro said to her 'Nice to meet you Maria' after which he stretched his hand to shake her hand. She shook his hand reluctantly as to say "is this guy here to stay, really?" and responded 'yeah alright'. He found it quite strange as that was not the response he expected. He didn't bring up how he waited for hours at the airport and Aunty Funke didn't bother making any apologies either. He just let sleeping dogs lie. He asked if he could have something to eat and she told him to warm up some food from the fridge. She later showed him his room... if you can call it that, and other things around the house.

As Duro went to bed that night, he realised that there was no fleet of cars, the house wasn't particularly a mansion, and there was no security guards everywhere. Those pictures weren't particularly as she may have painted them to be, he thought. And that rude Maria girl was probably going to be a challenge he was not really looking forward to at all.

Days became weeks and weeks turned into several months and still Aunty didn't make any mention of school or any kind of education for him. He saw Maria go to school every morning and saw her come back. He even ironed her school uniform for her on many occasions. Oh and as for shopping for new clothes as she had promised when she visited Nigeria, that was not even on the cards at all.

Aunty Funke had a little store room in the house which could only be accessed by her as she was the only one who had the keys. She often went out during the day time and came back late at night. No one, not even Maria knew what her Mum actually did for a living. Each day she will leave a list of things for Duro to do before she got back. He was always busy. From dish washing, hovering, ironing, folding clothes, gardening, to hand washing some of Auntie's clothes including her underwear. He barely had time to step out of the house. Most times, he ate amidst the loads of work he had to do. This was not the life he was promised. But could he summon enough courage to question Aunty? He didn't think so.

On a particular Saturday afternoon, Duro fell asleep on the couch after he had put the clothes out to dry. Aunty Funke was running late due to road closure on her way home. She had called the house phone a number of times but Duro was fast asleep. She realised that she had left the door to the 'secret store room' opened and was trying to call Duro so she could sternly warn him not to even think of going in there. When he eventually woke up he noticed that it was starting to drizzle. He quickly ran to the garden to take the clothes off the ropes that he had left out to dry. He wasn't ready to be told off again. The last time he forgot to bring them in when it drizzled, it wasn't a pleasant experience when Aunty Funke found out. Checking for messages on the house phone was the last thing on his mind. He ran around the house like some headless chicken to make up for the tasks he was yet to do before Aunty Funke arrived. Whilst he was vacuuming the corridors, he noticed the opened storage door and curiosity made him want to look inside. What is the worst that could happen? He thought. He pushed the door open a little bit more and then turned around and walked away really quickly.

Maria was not home yet. She was hardly home on Saturdays. Especially when she knew her Mum wouldn't be in for a long while. As soon as she got back home, she listened to the messages on the house phone after she noticed the notification lights blinking. She heard the message and headed straight for the storage room to find out what could be in there. Duro saw her 'tip toeing' her way to the storage room and tried to stop her but it was too late, she was already in. She turned on the lights just as Duro showed up behind her. They both beheld a very interestingly disturbing site. One they would have never imagined. A few seconds later, they heard the sound of a car parking outside the house. Aunty Funke had arrived. Turning the lights off, Maria ran to her room and Duro went to open the door to let Aunty in.

She pushed the door open, threw her bags to the floor and ran straight to the store room to check the state of it. She then asked if either of them had been in there. They both denied it. She locked the door and called for Duro. "Why were you not picking up the phone when I called? Are you deaf?" She yelled. "Sorry Aunty I fell asleep on the couch, I didn't hear the phone ring" he answered. "You must be very stupid, such a lazy thing you are, get lost". "But Aunty sorry I was tired; I didn't even know when I fell asleep." He replied. "How am I even sure you didn't go into the storage". Duro didn't respond. He just carried on with his work. "Am I not talking to you?" she asked. "I swear I didn't Aunty" Duro responded.

She asked if Maria had eaten and Maria somehow blamed Duro for not making her food. Duro faced another set of questioning after which he headed for the kitchen to prepare dinner. Whilst he served Aunty and Maria, he asked if he could have a brief discussion with Aunty after her dinner. She agreed.

Duro noticed that Aunty and Maria never really sat or spoke to each other. He found that mother-daughter relationship quite weird. Maria only spoke to her Mum when she needed money for shopping. And when her Mum refused, she would often storm out of the house but still came back with shopping bags. Her Mum hardly knew what Maria was up to and neither did Maria know much about her Mum. Duro stayed awake whilst he waited for his aunt to finish eating her food so they could have that discussion. Once she finished her meal, she was on the phone to one of her many friends. Duro waited a long while and she was still on the phone. He perambulated the sitting room a few more times but she still didn't take notice of him,. He went back to his room and waited some more until he eventually fell asleep.

From time to time Aunty Funke would call Elder Olu in Nigeria to talk about how well she was looking after Duro and that all was well. Sometimes, Duro overheard the conversations and wished he was allowed to speak. Elder Olu believed Aunty Funke. And who was he to question her words? After all, she sent money home so often to look after Elder Olu and his family. Why question 'the saviour'?

Chapter 6

That handsome fifteen year old was starting to look very haggard and had almost began to lose any amount of self-pride he had left after just two years of living with Aunty Funke. He was now seventeen years old. His hair was involuntarily turning into 'mini-dreadlocks'. You get the picture. He had done every task possible within the house. He had done his best to ensure that Aunty was happy with him. He already ran several errands both far and near distances. Still, every time he brought up his education, Aunty Funke often shrugged it off and said she would look into it. He often asked about his secondary school final exam results. Even that, was yet to be seen. Life in London for him was starting to become a nightmare. His dreams seemed to be running far away out of his reach.

He was on another of his many chores on this particular Saturday when Aunty Funke rang the house phone. To avoid getting told off by Aunty in case it was her, he ran as quickly as he could to reach the phone before it cut off. Panting heavily, he picked up. "Hello, hello, who is it?" Duro asked. "Why did it take you so long to get to the phone? You were not sleeping were you?" she asked. "No Aunty I actually wasn't". "Alright then, I want you to run a quick errand for me."

She then went ahead to instruct him on what to do. A few minutes later, Duro left what he was doing, went underneath his Aunty's bed and pulled out a tied black plastic bag and did not open it as warned by Aunty. He then headed for the specified destination. As he left the house running towards the bus stop as quickly as possible, he bumped into a young man, he apologised and kept running. Unknown to Duro, the plastic bag which was initially puffy, popped slightly on the side during the collision with the man. As he ran, the content from the bag began to leak unto the floor. It was quite a big plastic bag and it poured out continuously as he approached the bus stop which was quite a distance from his house. As he got closer to the bus stop, he looked behind and saw a trail of white coloured substance forming a wiggly line from where he had gone past. He immediately looked at his bag, saw it was still leaking out. He started getting unusual stares as he tried to hold the bag to stop it from leaking, a few seconds later, he noticed a couple of police officers on patrol from afar feeling the substance and smelling it. As they did, they looked ahead, pointed towards him and began to walk towards him. It was too far a distance to get to him very quickly. He smelt trouble. There was definitely something not right with what he was carrying. Immediately, without much hesitation, he found a nearby bin, threw the bag into it and began the race of his life. He ran as far as possible with all the energy he had within him.

He ran through the fields, through the back garden of strangers, he ran and ran some more. He eventually found his way back home after about another 30 minutes of running. On his arrival back to the house, Aunty was already back. She realised he came through the door in a rush, drenched in his own sweat and panting heavily. "Who's chasing you? I know I asked you to be quick but I don't remember telling you to run like some crazy man." She waited for a response but he was still trying to catch his breath. She continued "anyway, where's my money? I don't have time for all your drama today". Duro stood there for a while whilst he used his already wet brown T-shirt to rub the sweat off his face. "Aunty please can I drink some water?" clapping her hands together, she stood up responding in amazement "what does me asking for my money have anything to do with you drinking water? I don't see you with the bag I asked you to deliver. So I guess you got the payment in exchange for what you gave the man I sent you to?" Duro became dumbfounded. "Are you deaf, am I not talking to you?" she asked. Duro trying to answer her began to stutter. Where would he even begin his story? Should he lie? Would Aunty even believe his story? Can he even get away with this one? These many questions ran through his mind. He fell to his knees with his hands in a pleading gesture towards Aunty. "Ma I don't know what to say, I'm so sorry. I am really sorry, Errm, eh, Ahh sorry Aunty." With vigorous anger she shouted "sorry for what exactly, you idiot!" Duro then went ahead to explain what happened whilst he stayed on his knees. As he explained, Aunty got even more furious as she paced through the sitting room. Her eyes had turned red now at the thought of how much money she had lost. She interrupted him "do you even realise the effect of what you are saying? You threw over £7,000 worth of goods in the bin?" Duro answered "Aunty, I was scared; I didn't know what else to do..."Hitting him with the back of her palm, she responded. "Keep quiet and let me finish." She continued. "So I bring you to London to give your wretched orphan self a better life and this is how you pay me back?" Duro still on his knees dreaded what may happen next. Aunty Funke got even more furious as she walked around the living room angrily. She picked up the TV remote control, took off her shoes and threw them at Duro. She then reached for the small ceramic flower vase above the fire place and dashed it towards his forehead. Duro wasn't able to protect himself early enough. The vase smashed on his head, and immediately it began to bleed. Aunty showed no remorse whatsoever. She walked away angrily and said "if I still see you here in a few minutes, you will see what I will do to you." She left Duro struggling on his knees trying to stop the bleeding with his palm. Duro perceived that more trouble was coming. He hurriedly got up and made his escape from the house as quickly as he could. He walked to the park close to the house and sat under the trees where he tied his bleeding forehead with his T-shirt to stop any more blood loss. Going back to Aunty was like going back into the den of some angry and hungry lion. He was not ready for such a move. Besides, it would take a long while for her to calm down. It began to get really cold, temperature dropping to about two degrees Celsius and the night began to draw near. He had sat under that tree for hours. He stunk of a combination of sweat mixed with blood. His belly began to rumble too; he was hungry. At about 10pm that night, his phone rang. He looked at the screen to see who it was. Aunty Funke was calling. He eagerly picked up the call hopeful that he may actually spend the night in a warm bed. "Hello Duro, where is Maria? Do you know where she went?" she asked. "Errm no aunty, she didn't say where she was going." he replied. "Okay bye" she responded and hung up. After the very brief phone call from Aunty, for a few minutes, he was very puzzled for many reasons. Why didn't she ask where he was, if he was okay?

At that point, he knew there was no warm bed for him that night. He walked around the park to find his sleeping spot for the night. It felt like the longest night ever but he eventually closed his eyes to sleep and soon enough, dusk turned to dawn. He was woken up by the sound of his phone ringing. It was Aunty again. Maybe she eventually decided to care. He thought. He picked up. "Duro where are you? Come home now!" she shouted and hung up. He so was not looking forward to this kind of 'going home' not after she used that kind of tone. He thought what could have happened now. There was definitely 'fire on the mountain' now. He dusted himself off and made his way back to Aunty's house with his heart full of a truck load of fear. He didn't know what to expect.

Chapter 7

On getting back to the House, he saw Maria on the sofa with tears coming down her face. He had hardly ever seen her cry. He had seen her when she was moody for so many silly reasons but not this bad. Duro moved closer to her, sat beside her to find out if she was alright.

As he moved close to Maria, Aunty stormed down the stairs angrily into the living room. "Will you get your hands off my daughter? Haven't you done enough evil to this family?" Duro jumped off the sofa and leaned against the wall trying so hard to keep his calm. Aunty moved closer to him and carried on talking whilst she sipped a glass of gin. "Ohh Duro, now you have crossed the line. You will pay dearly for what you have done". Duro became even more confused. Is she still mad about the bag of cocaine he threw in the bin when he panicked when he was spotted by the police? Or has something worse happened that he was not aware of? "Why are you looking at me like you're some innocent boy? You had the audacity to touch my daughter?" she asked. Duro turned looking at both Aunty and Maria, very confused "Aunty I don't know what you are talking about, I'm baffled." He replied. "You forced my daughter to have sex with you didn't you? Now she's pregnant. Were you crazy or something?" She responded. Duro fell to his knees and spoke with all the sincerity he could. "Aunty, why would I do that? She's lying. Maria, please tell her it's not true. Maria please do not do this. Aunty Funke please, believe me even if it's only this once." He cried uncontrollably as he pleaded his case. However Aunty wasn't moved by his tears. She even got angrier as he spoke. Maria sat there still feeling sorry for herself but wouldn't say anything in Duro's presence. Aunty sipped more of her gin and she spoke some more, "How dare you rape my daughter!" She dashed the glass of gin towards him. Luckily for him, it brushed swiftly across his forehead, missed him and smashed against the wall. It was at that moment when Duro wished it was some April fool's prank that was being played on him at the wrong time. A few seconds later, there was a bang on the door. The police arrived to arrest Duro. Aunty had called them to report a case of rape suffered by her daughter supposedly inflicted by Duro.

Duro spent the entire day at the police station, locked in a cell before he was later brought out for questioning. Maria was interviewed separately. During her interview, she was critically interrogated and Officer Jenkins, her interviewer, was beginning to find issues with her story. She mentioned that she had a boyfriend. Well more like a 'Man friend', in his early thirties. She also said he had been one of the sexual partners she had been involved with in recent times. She talked about how intimidating he was and how he refused to accept that she was pregnant with his baby and threatened to hurt her if she mentioned it to anyone as she had no proof. She also explained that she was too scared to tell her Mum that she was pregnant for a grown man. She got scared and blamed it on the already hated victim, Duro. She didn't know her Mum would have involved the police. Once she made the statement, the police had no reason to hold Duro any longer, so he was released.

He made up his mind that nothing in this world would make him return to Aunty Funke's house. Not long after he left East Ham police station, his phone rang. Again, it was Aunty. He ignored her call a few times. But she kept calling. He eventually picked up. "Duro I want you to come home now from wherever you are". Her order sounded like gibberish to his ears. He wasn't ready to obey this time. He put himself together and answered her "Sorry Aunty, I won't be coming home."

Even Duro himself was shocked that he had uttered that statement. But he wasn't ready to change his mind. He spoke some more "Aunty every single day in your house has literally been like living in hell. I don't think I have wronged you in any way to be treated the way you have treated me. Aunty I've done so much for you, I just needed you to enroll me into some kind of education. For two years now, nothing! I know sometimes life in itself isn't fair, but with you, it's worse than it's supposed to be. Aunty Funke, I've had enough. I'm not stepping a foot in that house of yours." After hearing him lament, she paused for a few seconds and then burst out in laughter. Then she responded "You think you are smart but you forget that your life here depends on me. I'm sure you don't know you have overstayed your visa here. If I don't see you at home in the next 24hours, I will call the UK Border Agency and report you as an Illegal resident. Hope you understand the repercussion of that you Idiot".

"Aunty I understand." Duro replied. Aunty added "you know if you get caught. You are going to be deported straight back to Nigeria to face a life of misery. So if you know what is good for you, make your way to the house now." Duro simply responded, "Sorry Aunty, not this time. Bye Aunty" and he hung up the phone. Aunty Funke was shocked, she never heard him speak like that. It felt as though he had lost every reverence he had ever had for her. She had lost her grip on him. She tried to call him again but she could not get through, he did not pick up. She sent him a text threatening to burn his passport and secondary school final exam results. Duro was shocked to read this. He was never told that Elder Olu had already sent his school results. He did not know how he did in the exams he worked so extremely hard for. But this was not going to make him return to her house. He wasn't afraid anymore. Now he was all alone, he didn't have any friends to speak of. Where would he have met them really? He definitely would not have found them while he was at home doing endless chores and countless errands. The only option he could think of was his neighbour but that was too close to Aunty. For one of the very few times in his life, he had to stand his ground. He knew he didn't have it all figured out but he was ready to face each day after the other. He thought of calling Elder Olu in Nigeria, but he had no credit on the phone to make such a call. As he walked along various streets, passersby looked at him with pity. He was dirty and had started to smell unpleasant. He headed to the local park again, found a spot there underneath a tree and before long, he dozed off.

For several days, he walked to various places, hoping to get some sort of menial job to make enough money to buy a meal. At times when he couldn't get such jobs, he kindly asked passersby to spare a change. He had to survive somehow, he was starting to lose weight and dirt was very visible on his skin. He had not had a bath for several days. Many times when he sat to rest, he would question himself as to why he didn't stand his ground more when the offer to live with Aunty Funke was put to him. How did things get so bad so quickly? Why was Aunty so mean? Of course he had no answers to any of these questions. Surviving each day as it came was the only thing on his mind. More days went by and the weather started to change drastically. It got colder and most nights were wet, and this made it totally unbearable to sleep underneath trees as he would normally do. So, he devised another method to find a comfortable space to sleep. He began to sneak into the local bus garage, and then sneak into one of the night buses right after the cleaners cleaned it just before the bus door would shut. At the early hours of the morning as the driver began his shift, he would sneak out. He did this for many nights; he made the bus his bedroom.

Chapter 8

One particular evening, as he went on his walks, he noticed people coming out of a large gate and some others going in, it was a big building. It looked like a warehouse. He went closer to get some information on what the place was about. He found out that they were factory workers. It was a candle factory. Some workers were finishing their shift and some going in to start a new shift. He walked in with the staff beginning their shift. He walked round asking for the manager or the team leader. He later met him and straightaway literally begged to work there for whatever wage he was offered. The manager stated that he was not hiring and he didn't need a new worker. Duro promised that he would do all he could. He even offered to do night shifts and long hours. He really needed this. The manager saw desperation in his eyes; he was moved to help him. He gave him the night shift and said he could begin that same night. Duro was ecstatic at this opportunity. At least now he could earn some money and he had a place to go every night which was definitely better than his 'night bus bedroom'. For each night shift he worked there, he was paid £14.22. This was so little compared to the wages of the rest of the workers but he couldn't complain. He really did not have the legal documents to work, so really, the manager employed him out of pity. He made a couple of new friends of which some allowed him to have showers in their houses from time to time. He barely had enough sleep every night. Sometimes he offered to help the manager lock up after the night shift just so he could squeeze in a few hours of sleep before the morning shift staff arrive.

He spent most of the daytime in the library. From there, he often found out about opportunities in the local area or in neighbouring boroughs. He spent a lot of time reading. As time went by, he had read most of the major books in the library. He also read a lot of business journals, financial magazines and a lot of newspapers. He realised that from time to time, after long night shifts, he got really tired. He felt that for a young man his age, he was not as fit or agile as he believed he ought to be. He asked if there was some sort of free fitness club around. He kept asking the librarian for several weeks until she was able to enquire about a free athletics club for 'under 18s' which was a few miles away from the library. He was just under 18 years old at the time and was still eligible to join. He joined and utilised a lot of his free time during the day to exercise; exercise then became training. He wasn't sure what he was training for but he pushed himself nonetheless. He soon became very popular amongst the instructors and coaches and because of the dedication that they saw in him, they convinced him to enter into programs and events. He excelled at many events and was entered for several inter-borough decathlon competitions.

Duro had also missed going to church. Aunty Funke really never went. She only went to church if it happened to be on her birthday, Christmas and on New Year's Day. She felt for some reason she needed to be close to God on those days. However, on other days, she didn't see much need to go. When Duro was in Nigeria before Mama passed away, they never missed Sunday services and mid-week services. Mama was the leader of the Elders group, she loved church and her love for it rubbed off on Duro. Now, he felt the need to go back to how Mama trained him. He found a local church and began to attend consistently. He needed all the faith he could get, knowing his many predicaments. He got very involved and began to take on different responsibilities in his local church. Members referred to him as a remarkable and an exemplary young chap.

Duro kept his job at the candle factory for the years that followed. He eventually became a supervisor and his wages increased to a more reasonable amount. He had saved enough money to be able to get a shared room with one of his close mates at the factory. He also continued his athletics although he was now in the under 25s category. The competition was tougher now so he had to work even harder. But now that he was a supervisor, he had less time to practise because of his factory supervisory responsibilities. He also worked some daytime shifts when asked. Every little bit helped. Despite the stiff competition in the club, he still maintained very excellent performance but soon started to have rivals. He was shortlisted as a sprinter for the Annual Nation-wide competitions sponsored by a major telecommunications company. I'm sure his sprinting to school when he was much younger had a thing or two to do with his running skills. He was shortlisted alongside another member of the athletic club, Adrian. Adrian was highly competitive. He hated losing and did not like seeing others who he considered his equal challenge his ability. And he saw Duro as a threat!

The day for the competition was finally upon them and the arena was packed out with excited spectators ready to cheer on the enthusiastic athletes taking part in the highly anticipated series of events.

The events kicked off and several heats for the sprint category also took place. Duro eased through the qualifying stages but was often behind Adrian by just a fraction of a second.
The time for the semi-finals in the 100m sprint men category came. Duro, other athletes and of course Adrian approached the track and were cheered on by the spectators. Adrian approached Duro, nudged him on the shoulder and whispered into his ears. Duro kept his calm and didn't react. It just so happened that their running lanes was also right next to each other. Duro was on lane 4

and Adrian on lane 5. The gun was shot and the race began. Each sprinter giving it all they had, they had to make the finals; there was really no great margin between each sprinter. The pressure was high, everyone pulling out all the skills, styles and strength within them. As they got closer to the finish line, Duro slightly began to pull ahead of Adrian. Adrian couldn't catch up in time; hence he put his foot forward to throw Duro off balance. Duro tripped and fell face down. Before, he could get up to carry on; other athletes had dashed ahead to the finish line including Adrian. Duro got right up, went after Adrian, put his hand on his neck, pushed him to the ground and a fight evolved with punches thrown and several bruises in the process. Officials ran to the track to intervene and attempt to stop the fight. The whole competition was disrupted for about 25 minutes and it carried on after Duro and Adrian were taken off the track by the officiating police to be questioned.

On getting to the police station, they were both asked to identify themselves and provide any form of ID. This was a challenge for Duro. He had overstayed his visa in the country and had absolutely no form of ID on him. The police decided to call the Home Office to check up on his records. The Home Office confirmed that his six months visiting visa had expired a long time ago and that he was an 'over stayer' who had disregarded the immigration rules and should be taken into detention as soon as possible. The police were told to keep him in a cell until a van was able to come and pick him up later that evening. Adrian on the other hand was released with a warning. He had sufficient ID on him. Duro was led by a police officer into a cell where he spent the rest of the day until the Home Office van arrived. As he made the loneliest walk ever towards the cell, the metallic silver handcuff on his wrists made an annoying dangling noise with every step he took. It was a very terrible moment for him. In a foreign land, and now being tagged a supposed 'criminal'. If taking his life was an option presented to him at that moment, he probably would have given it some consideration. The fear of being forcefully removed from the UK was there. But the real fear was the fear of being traumatised by extended family in Nigeria who may have thought he caused Aunty so much trouble based on the tales she may have told them. He sat in his cell in deep thought until he dozed off.

Chapter 9

-Number 10 to Number 10-

The Home office van arrived later that evening. He was woken up and escorted into a white van alongside two other detainees. There was a metallic bar mesh that separated the detainees seats from the driver and assisting officer. There was also a little flap on the metal mesh where they spoke to the detainees from time to time. Duro asked where they were being taken to and he was told somewhere in Portsmouth. He had never been there. What was a detention centre like? Is it some sort of prison? No one really knew his whereabouts. What if he gets removed to Nigeria? These many questions popped up in his mind as he traveled for a long time. He was so desperate for a miracle. The thought of him being removed to Nigeria disturbed him greatly. Aunty must have told them a lot of lies that many would have perceived him as such an ungrateful orphan. He was not ready for that life of misery. He had no phone on him; it was taken off him when arrested. The money he had on him was taken too. All he had was a little bit of hope in his pocket. He had lost all appetite now, what would happen when he got out of the van was what was on his mind. The van eventually got to Portsmouth and arrived at Haslar Immigration Removal Centre which was for male detainees. He couldn't but notice the really high metallic security gates and surrounding thick concrete and metal walls with barbed wires. The van went through different security checks at each gate before it got to the building. Duro thought within himself how that one moment of him reacting in anger led to him being in that prison-like environment. The time of arrival was around 11.30pm at night. He had a quick induction, medical test, his detainee card was printed and a detainee number allocated to him. He was offered something to eat but he turned it down. He was taken down the hallway and shown to his dormitory and his room which he would share with three others. He was put in room number 10 in Dormitory A. He was very tired and laid on the bottom part of the dark grey-coloured metal bed to get some rest after such a traumatic day and long journey. Just before he fell asleep he said a prayer as simply as he could. If he was going to leave that place, it would take a miracle. He closed his eyes that night in earnest hope that he would wake up to a reality of freedom and not in that enclosed environment. Morning seem to come too soon. He opened his eyes and yes he was very much still in the detention centre. There was a great deal to get used to. The lunch and dinner times were fixed, the dormitory gates also shut at a certain time. The staff were mostly prison officers. Duro had not been to prison before but he believed the Immigration detention centre was not very far off from being a prison. Each morning,

Duro would look out the room window and all he would see was really high security fences, many feet high. He longed to see beyond the walls. He longed to see his newly made friends from the factory. Of course he tried to stay strong, never forgetting to pray as he was taught by Mama Ajibade and as he had learnt from church also. Each day he would enquire if there was any sort of legal help for him. Many times he was told there wasn't. But he remained hopeful. After about 4 days, he began to get used to the routine, he got some change of clothes, beddings, and slippers from the laundry section. He never stopped enquiring for some legal help. He asked different officials and one day he was told by one of them of a visit by a couple of lawyers sent by a charity to help detainees with little or no legal representation. On the afternoon when the lawyers were scheduled to visit, he was at the entrance of the interview room thirty minutes before they arrived. He was the first detainee they met with that day. He explained his situation to them and they discussed the possible options he had. Mr Jimmy Hawkins decided he would take on Duro's case. A couple of days after he met with them, they put in a bail application in hopes of it possibly leading to a bail hearing.

The centre was occupied by people from diverse races and culture mostly from different parts of Africa and Asia. He had heard different stories as to how many people found themselves in there. Some had been there for months and some for over a year. A few others had even taken on jobs within the centre to earn some money whilst they were there. Each detainee got £1 as allowance for each day they spent there. He spent most of his time in the centre's library and other times he sat on the bunk bed in the room he shared and expressed himself in writing. He wrote about his experiences, he wrote about the hope he had of being released. That was the only way he knew how to let out his emotions. There was no one to cry to. But every time he put his pen to paper, he was speaking to himself and talking himself out of that place.

Duro's writing in detention centre

Same people everywhere
(coded letter to the rude security guard)

I have concluded my thought process of initially thinking that people were different. They say those who live in the western world are supposedly more polite or more caring than those in less developed countries. In a nut shell, that is a lie. People are the same, just in different shapes, colours, speech variation and in different circumstances.

If these people are put in the same circumstances, faced with the same challenges, exposed to the same information, they would all react the same way and come out with the same results. So not

88

for one second, try to tell me people are different.
They are exactly the same.

The same 'more courteous western people' treat
you funny once they get a glimpse that they have
a little power over you; even if on a normal day,
they realised that they don't match up to you.
Now, the security guards speak to you roughly
just because they think you are some kind of
offender although you have been unfairly judged.
Let's never forget that the actions we take, our
treatment of people, the way we speak of others is
an amplifier of the person inside. Before you
become a monster, start by remembering that
people are the same everywhere and just because
you were born in a western country does not
make you superior.

Smile through it

DJ Lopez, the self-made dormitory DJ is such a joker. He breaks every rule possible but is still loved by many. He even has his own separate room now. His loud music disturbs everyone but no one complains. After all, he helps liven up this place.

Then we have the loud ones, the rude ones- who change the TV channel without the courtesy to ask others. Well, 'his people' outnumbered me, so he felt very confident to change it to his own native station although I sat there before him. Shall I speak my mind or go and change it myself or should I just let him be. Well, I walked away and smiled. It's not my TV anyway, so why fight over it. If he wants to feel at home, that's his business. For me, I choose not to get too comfortable here.

So much banter, so many funny characters. I seize every opportunity to laugh as hard as I can. I don't let them go. After all, laughter does good as medicine.

The King in Me

I may be locked up in some place with high fences, barbed wires and cameras everywhere. The food I eat, what I wear and even the type of deodorant I use are decided for me. I have to eat this food even though I'm not sure what it is and all I crave for is some spicy wings from the shop down my street. That for now, is luxury.

The people I talk to, the room I sleep in, the times the gates shut and when the corridor lights go off may be controlled. Even when I see who I choose to see may be controlled. All these may be controlled but the king in me still reigns.

My physical body may be restricted but my mind travels beyond the fences and barbed wires and strong metal gates. Oh boy! My spirit cannot be restricted. I can see a greater life outside of this place.

Each day, as I pray, sing and study my Bible, the king in me arises. It's not long anymore, a day closer, an hour closer, a minute closer, a second closer, this king's body will no longer be restricted. He will reign and rule as he was destined to. He will teach others to be independent of circumstances.

I can see the king in me arising and in no time, his life will be a testimony of faith, favor, fear-deficient, patience, perseverance and prayer.

The king in me can't be restrained, He's got to come out and do what he was born to do, Reign!

Knocked out? Never!

*It doesn't matter how many times I get punched,
It doesn't matter how many times I lost in the
past. I am stronger now, I am wiser now.*

*It's my time now!
I know I will win now.
Hope you enjoyed your past victories, sorry they
were short lived.
I rub my palms in excitement as I anticipate my
victory and celebration.*

*I anticipate that my testimony will stir up hope in
others
You can't knock me out this time
I can see myself grinning with joy, it's my time
now. Not yours!*

I won

Written days before his bail hearing date

I told you I was going to win
I told you this thing had to spit me out
I told you I was independent of the challenge
I told you God in me was greater than whatever
tried to challenge me.

I jumped over the hurdles
I kept the faith
I remained hopeful
I never took my eyes off the prize
Can't wait to get to noisy, buzzy London
Can't wait to see my friends again
Can't wait!
Can't wait to change lives and prove to all one
more time that God's word always works.

Around 12.30 pm on a Monday afternoon, as Duro was on the queue for lunch, he heard his name on the public announcement speakers. He was asked to come to the centre's office. He immediately jumped out of the queue to enquire as to why he was being called. He was handed a letter with his name on it. He opened it right there to find out what was in there. He tore open the envelope and began to read the content of the letter. He jumped up in excitement. His bail hearing application was approved and he was given a hearing date.

He smiled his way back to the canteen to have lunch. He remained hopeful. After lunch, he rang his lawyer to please help ensure that one of his friends from the candle factory and another from his local church, whose names were submitted as sureties on the bail application attended the bail hearing with the required documents. The lawyer assured him that he would make contact with them.

The hearing date was the Friday morning of that same week. Duro would have to join via a live video-link connection. He would watch the whole court proceedings on a screen and will speak via a headset microphone if he is questioned about anything. He was ready an hour before the 10.30am hearing. He paced around the corridors full of anticipation as he waited for the door to the viewing room to be opened. He had been in the detention centre for three long months. He had had enough. He hoped the result from this hearing could be his ticket out of that place.

The bail hearing commenced and he sat on the brown oak wooden chair as he stared at the screen in front of him not wanting to miss a word said by the judge, his lawyer or anyone in the court. He noticed his friend James and Brother Clement from church were present as his sureties. For the first 30 minutes of the hearing, everything seemed not to go in Duro's favour. The Home Office representative had everything negative he could say. They brought up the fact that he had been arrested by the police on two occasions. However his lawyer defended Duro and mentioned that the charge of rape concerning Maria was dropped as it was simply a false accusation. Also, he mentioned that the case of the fight that broke out during the athletics event was simply a response out of anger given the circumstance that led to the fight. On both grounds Duro was really not convicted of any crime and that he was clear of any criminal record. The Home Office representative brought up several other aspects of the law to ensure that Duro wasn't granted bail. However, Duro's lawyer did his utmost best to counter every point. Duro listened with rapt attention, with his legs shaking uncontrollably and palms getting sweaty quickly; His nerves had the better of him. Luckily for him, he was not questioned about anything at that time.

The judge then asked the Immigration lawyer if they had made a decision on what to do with him bearing in mind that he had been in detention for about three months. The Home Office representative responded "Errm, in actual fact, we are yet to decide". She then asked Duro's lawyer "Can you confirm Mr. Duro has any pending application?" and he responded "Yes your honour, he does". Duro thought he didn't hear well. He knew he didn't have any pending application. He was in a confused state.

The judge then gave her verdict. "Well this is a simple decision for me. Firstly, I am satisfied with the documents provided by the sureties and the amount of money they are willing to put down as security should Mr. Duro abscond. I must also say that I am absolutely appalled that the Home Office would detain someone for this length of time and your response is you are still thinking of what to do with him? It seems to me like some sort of indefinite detention. Seriously, I'm not a fan of that. More so, he has a pending application. I therefore do not see any reason for him to still be detained when there is no likelihood of him being removed anytime soon. I therefore order the immediate release of Mr. Duro. This hearing is over. I rise"

After the verdict was given, Duro fell to his knees with his hands lifted up in thanks to God. He was still surprised to know he had an application. He rang his lawyer to find out what actually happened in there and how did he get to have a pending application?

His lawyer, Mr. Jimmy explained to him about how the members of his church got financially involved and how they wanted to do all they could do to ensure that he was not forcefully removed. Following his suggestions, they put some money together and he was able to file an application for Duro bearing in mind he already had Duro's information, Immigration history and current circumstances when they had their initial interview and from numerous conversations over the phone.

Later that evening, Duro was released from Haslar detention centre. The centre covered his transport cost for him to make his way back from Portsmouth to Elephant and Castle station where he was able to make it home...even though it was a shared room, it was home for him.

About seven months following his release, the Home Office requested for his Nigerian passport before they could make a decision. His lawyer responded and informed them of his passport situation and explained how his Aunty had it with her and he had lost contact with her after he previously suffered numerous physical abuse and emotional abuse from her. A couple of weeks later, a letter was sent with the Home Office decision. They stated his immigration history, and also mentioned that they did not have enough identification documents for him whilst his application was being considered. They also added that they were not satisfied with the evidence presented to them and therefore do not see any valid reason why he should be allowed to remain in the country. However, he had a right to appeal the decision if necessary.

Mr. Jimmy was not pleased with the Home Office's response. Therefore, he advised that they asked for a reconsideration of the decision giving his reasons and circumstances. After another two weeks, the Home office responded but still maintained their decision.

The last trick Mr. Jimmy thought to pull out of the hat was to put in an appeal application to request a court hearing before an Immigration Judge.

Another month later, the appeal hearing was approved and a hearing date given. On the day of the hearing, Duro was suited up in a black suit, white shirt and a red tie. He did his best to look presentable. His friends from the candle factory, and some church members were there to support him also. The hearing began and both lawyers argued their cases. Mr. Jimmy was present however another Barrister who was more specialized in immigration law represented Duro. She put forward a really strong case explaining the trauma he had been through from his Aunty, she also detailed the fact that his parents passed away when he was a baby. He had no real family to look after him hence he was sent to the UK to live with his Aunty. And of course that didn't turn out great at all. She listed all the abuse he suffered and how being sent back home will be a torture as he had no real family ties there. She raised many more arguments in his defense. The Home Office lawyer raised her own argument as well, stating the same reasons that was stated in the initial refusal letter that was previously sent. It was a heated hearing and it eventually began to draw to a close. The judge allowed each lawyer to do a summary of their arguments before the judge concluded. He stated that he would need some time to look at all the documents and arguments presented to him before he can arrive at a reasonably fair conclusion.

Four weeks later, Duro was heading to the library as he normally did whenever he happened to have an easy day. His phone rang. It was his lawyer. Duro was already hoping that he would hear from him all week. He hurriedly picked up the call. Mr Jimmy asked him to come and see him at his office as soon as he possibly could and he responded "okay" and the conversation ended. Duro stood for a few seconds and wondered why the conversation was that brief and why Mr Jimmy didn't say much. Duro began panicking. He had had enough of battling the Home Office for that length of time. He tried calling Mr Jimmy back but he was not getting through. Duro began his journey to his lawyer's office.

On getting there, he was told that Mr Jimmy was in the meeting room with a client. He waited for about thirty minutes and his lawyer was ready to see him. As he stepped into his office, Mr Jimmy keeping a straight face pushed an envelope across the table towards Duro. He wasn't ready for any more bad news at this time. Mr Jimmy typed away on his computer as Duro nervously opened the letter and doing it as slowly as possible as he was unsure of its content. He pulled out the papers stapled together and he began to read the letter. It contained the decision from the judge following the appeal hearing.

Duro read the letter speedily so as to get to the conclusion at the end of the letter and the eventual decision the judge arrived at. As he approached the last few paragraphs, he fell to his knees, dropped the letter on the floor and raised his hands in total awe. His face lit up with so much joy, it could almost brighten a dark cave. The judge had decided the case in his favour. He was granted indefinite leave to remain in the UK. He ran around the table hugged Mr Jimmy and thanked him wholeheartedly. This meant a lot to him. He didn't need Aunty Funke any longer for whatsoever reason. He wasn't going to be deported. He didn't have to face the grief and shame from extended family members. He could study, he could work legally. He had some freedom in his life. Now he could see a tiny ray of light ahead. He left Mr. Jimmy's office walking on air. He was elated. He had a future!

Duro already had a lot of information on education, what colleges he could go to, what universities he could possibly attend afterwards and the courses to study. He immediately began his application process to enroll on a level 3 intensive access course to qualify for university. However he needed his secondary school leaving certificate and exam results. He thought of seeing Aunty but he wasn't ready mentally or emotionally to see her yet. After a couple of days of thinking,

105

he thought of an idea. He took to social media to find his close friend whilst he was in Ejigbo, Lagos. He searched for his friend, Oluchi. Of course he had to sieve through several similar names but he eventually found the Oluchi he was looking for. He began communicating with her and they exchanged messages from time to time. He asked her to help him contact his secondary school and to have them please provide copies of his results and school leaving certificate. She promised that she would do all she could to make it happen. She did. Two weeks later, she posted them to him which allowed him to enroll into his chosen course at college.

On completion of his course after two years, Duro enrolled and began his university degree at the age of 24. He studied Economics at the University of Leicester. Duro knew how long he waited to get into education; hence he wasn't one of those who joked around. He took each lecture seriously and wrote each exam as though it was his last one. He was extremely diligent. He got involved with the student union in his university and was voted President of the student union after a couple of months. University in all, was a tough experience for him, he was just getting used to the education system in the UK after his 2 years of College. He also took interest in politics and joined a political party whilst he was still in his second year of university. Duro painstakingly worked on his final year projects and even had an internship at the office of the Councillor of the Exchequer. He began to build a wealth of experience and knowledge. Soon after his graduation with a First Class Honours degree in Economics, his influence began to increase in the party he joined whilst he was still a student, the Labour party. He was then 29 years of age and only a couple of months to his 30th birthday. He had given a lot of ideas to the party which they had implemented and he climbed up the ranks quicker than any expected. It was all happening so quickly. Rumour had it that he was probably going to be implored to be the new party leader as the party needed something new, unique and dynamic. From his life experience and witty initiatives, a lot of personalities within the political party had their eyes on this almost 30 year old young man to save them at the next elections.

Many months went by and the General elections eventually took place. Duro mounted the podium dressed in a navy blue bespoke tailored pinstriped suit, white shirt complimented with a red tie. He was welcomed by cheers from the audience as various news reporters had their camera lights flashing, different microphones and recording devices pointed towards the podium. In many homes, people sat in front of their television screens paying absolute concentrated attention, television stations from around the world were covering this event. From the villages, to cites, offices to market squares, in every nook and cranny people watched. No one wanted to miss this history-making moment of the Inaugural speech from the first Black Prime minister of the United Kingdom.

The whole world was quiet as he opened his mouth to utter his first few words. You could literally hear a pin drop. They had waited so long for that moment.

Duro began to speak.

"Today is much more than a black man being the Prime minister of this nation. It's about celebrating hope, celebrating faith and celebrating the win of many fights, the fight to be somebody! It's about how a little boy from the streets of Lagos Nigeria had a simple dream to grow up and live a comfortable life just as we all strive for. But things really never turn out the way you dream without challenges and a bit of fighting. I never met my parents. They were brutally killed when I was still a few months old. I lost the only people who were ever there for me, my grandparents. Things turned out worse than I could ever hope. I don't have to dig too deep into history now as I suppose many of you already read or heard about my background already."

As he spoke, he was interrupted by rousing applauses from the audience who listened intently.

He carried on speaking.

"...with all the strength within me, I want to emphasise that a man's current situation does not have anything to do with where he is headed. If he can see success, he can be it. I know our beloved country at this time is undergoing a lot of hardship and challenges. We are facing terror threats from certain nations and of course our economy needs a lot of fixing up at this time also. But I am here now, hope has come, the solution has come. All my life, I have faced a lot of unbearable challenges and I believe I am ready for whatever life has to throw at me. Many who did not even face half of what I faced growing up have been unable to cope. But I have a thick skin, a witty mind and unparalleled resilience. In my time, the United Kingdom will prosper, will make friends and not enemies and overall, we will re-instate the 'Great' back into 'Great Britain.' We will become a force to reckon with one more time."

Loud applauses again interrupted his speech.

"If nothing else inspires you, I bet you will be inspired by the real story of a young man who was detained in Room number 10 of an Immigration detention centre and now in House Number 10 Downing Street, as Prime minister - same number, but different locations."

"...Well, a lot of people know me as Duro. But that is the short form of my name 'Aduroja'; the one who can stand a fight, the man who doesn't run from a fight, the man who doesn't know how to throw in the towel, and the man who doesn't stop until he wins. You can call me Undisputed!"

SOME EVENTS AND LOCATIONS WHERE SAMSON HAS BEEN A SPEAKER

- West Africa, Nigeria- Success Motivation Youth Conference.

- House of Lords & House of Commons, Houses of Parliament, United Kingdom- UK Youth Parliament Debate

- Schools in London, United Kingdom

- Television and Online- Guest Expert on different   talk shows

- Microsoft, London –Youth Delegate

- National Youth week event – United Kingdom

- Community Teenagers Conference, South East England

- Brixton, United Kingdom- promoting   sexual health/HIV/AIDS awareness

- Shine Youth Conference- England, 2012

- 'You Can' Young People's Event, London, 2013

- Lewisham Schools Award

- Young Managers Board Event, South East England

- Spokesperson during a BBC interview for Young people's view on National ID cards

- Black History Month Inspirational speaker, South East London, United Kingdom

- Cedar Leadership Business conference Heathrow, London

- Kwame Nkrumah University of Science and Technology, Ghana, 2015

- Orphanage homes in West Africa, 2015

- 'The Xtra-ordinary Youth Summit 2015 London, United Kingdom

Some of Samson's other volunteering achievements & Awards

- Author of 'Lessons From my Father', 'Undisputed' & 'Sally's Surprise'
- Samson has done well over two thousand hours of volunteering
- Gold Duke of Edinburgh Award: On the 8th April 2009
- Youth Member of Parliament for Lewisham in the United Kingdom Youth parliament
- Campaigned against Child Poverty
- Member of the Lewisham Young Managers Board
- Young Citizen's Award
- Youth Affairs Director at a Charity
- Youth Advisory Board member for Dare London (London Youth and Greater London Authority)
- Student of the Year Awards
- Judging panel on National Crimebeat Awards

- Philanthropic acts to orphanages

Contact Information:

I will appreciate hearing from you. I look forward to hearing your views, comments and testimonials.

Write to me or contact me on the details below:

Website: www.speak2samson.co.uk
E-mail: speak2samson@gmail.com

Find me on
Facebook: Samson Adeyemi
Follow my page *'SamTheGreat' on Facebook*
Twitter: @speak2sam
Linked-In: Samson Adeyemi
YouTube: www.youtube.com/speak2samson

I look forward to hearing from you.

Samson M. Adeyemi